This book is dedicated to Mrs. Harriet Lucia,
my second grade teacher at Southwest Elementary School in Grand Rapids, Minnesota.
Mrs. Lucia taught every student the importance of being kind and helpful toward others,
as well as the importance of imagination. It is because of good teachers like her
that children grow to be dreamers, thinkers, and helpful citizens.

And to every child who has ever dared to imagine what they would do
should a moose want to be their best friend—may you someday have the chance to find out.

—K. J. W.

For my huge family and as ever, my wonderful wife, Tiziana.

—J. B. B.

Sleeping Bear Press™

2395 South Huron Parkway, Suite 200
Ann Arbor, MI 48104

www.sleepingbearpress.com

Printed and bound in the United States.

16 15 14 13 12 11

Library of Congress Cataloging-in-Publication Data

Wargin, Kathy-jo.
Moose on the loose / written by Kathy-jo Wargin ; illustrated by John Bendall-Brunello.
p. cm.
Summary: Rhyming text poses a series of questions about how the reader would deal with a
moose that is on the loose, in the yard, in the house, or taking a bath.
ISBN 978-1-58536-427-5
[1. Stories in rhyme. 2. Moose—Fiction. 3. Humorous stories.] I. Bendall-Brunello, John, ill. II. Title.
PZ8.3.W2172Moo 2009
[E]—dc22
2009004803

Moose
on the
Loose

Kathy-jo Wargin

Illustrated by

John Bendall-Brunello

Sleeping Bear Press™

PUBLISHER

What would you do with a **moose** on the **loose?**

Would you
chase him,
or **race** him, or
stand up to **face** him?

What would you do
with a **moose** on the **loose?**

What would you do
with a **moose** in
your **yard?**

NO
MOOSE
HERE

Would you ask for a **ride**
or invite him to **slide?**
What would you do
with a **moose** in your **yard?**

What if that moose
came to live in your house?
Would you read him a book?
Would you teach him to cook?

Would you ask him to **dance**?

Would you dress him in **pants**?

What would you do with a moose in your house?

Now what if that **moose** went upstairs to your room?

Would you beat him at chess?
Would he make a big mess?

Would you ask him to **sing** and then crown him as **king?**

What if that moose
started wearing
your SOCKS?

Would you **cry**?
Would you **yell**?
Would you tell him
they **smell**?

Would you give
him two more
and then bid him
farewell?

And what if that **moose** took a bath in your **tub**?

Would you give him two boats?
Would you see if he floats?

Would you towel him **dry**?
Would you tell him don't **cry**?

Would you find him **pajamas** and then feed him **pie**?

What if that **moose**
went to sleep in your **bed**?
Would you tuck him in **tight**?
Would you kiss him
goodnight?

Would you plump
up his pillow
and turn out the
light?

Would you tickle
his **toes?**
Would you pinch
at his **nose?**

Would you shout, "this is it! You are too big to fit!"

And what if that **moose** says to you the next **day**, "I think I will **stay**."

Would you
chase him **away**?
Would you say it's **OK**?

Then go ask your
mother–
she has the last **say**.